BASEBALL KIDS

BASEBALL KIDS

George Sullivan

Illustrated with photographs

COBBLEHILL BOOKS Dutton New York

ACKNOWLEDGMENTS

The author is grateful to the many players and coaches who helped in the preparation of this book. Special thanks are due Alan Hubbard and Tom Mineo, coaches of the East Longmeadow Cardinals; Gilbert Caraballo, manager of the Love Gospel Assembly Hurricanes, and coach Jose Rosario; also, Mary and Bob Mazzariello, Francesca Kurti, TLC Custom Labs, and Aime LaMontagne.

All photographs are by George Sullivan.

Library of Congress Cataloging-in-Publication Data
Sullivan, George, date
Baseball kids/George Sullivan.
p. cm.
Summary: Profiles twelve boys, ages eleven to thirteen, who play baseball, revealing their likes and dislikes, favorite plays, and individual views of the game.
ISBN 0-525-65023-7
1. Baseball for children—United States—Juvenile literature. 2. Baseball players—United States—Biography—Juvenile literature. [1. Baseball players.] I. Title.
GV880.4.S85 1990 796.357'092'2—dc20 [B] [920] 89-29102 CIP AC

Published in the United States by Cobblehill Books,
an affiliate of Dutton Children's Books, a division
of Penguin Books USA Inc.
Published simultaneously in Canada by
Fitzhenry & Whiteside Limited, Toronto
Designed by Jean Krulis
Printed in the U.S.A.
First Edition 10 9 8 7 6 5 4 3 2 1

CONTENTS

Introduction 7

MIKE ST. CLAIR
Pitcher, Shortstop 9

PAT CAMPBELL
Left Field, Third Base 16

OMAR RAMIREZ
Second Base, Third Base, Pitcher 23

PAT HELLYER
Second Base, Catcher 29

DAN DESILETS
Left Field, Center Field, Second Base 37

BRIAN KARAVISH
Third Base, First Base 43

SENECA PEREZ
Center Field 48

TOM MINEO
First Base, Pitcher 56

STEVEN MAZZARIELLO
Shortstop, Second Base, Pitcher 65

STEVEN BAEZ ROSARIO
Shortstop, Outfield, Pitcher 74

ALAN HUBBARD
Catcher, Pitcher 80

CHRIS CONWAY
Second Base 87

Glossary 92

Index 94

INTRODUCTION

Kids don't play children's games any more," says Dr. Glyn C. Roberts, a professor at the Institute of Child Behavioral Development at the University of Illinois. "They're more likely to play childlike versions of adult sports, such as shooting baskets or throwing a football.

"Sports skills," says Dr. Roberts, "have generally supplanted what used to be general playing skills."

With most youngsters, nothing beats playing baseball. At six and seven, they're playing tee ball, a baseball-type game. Not only are they capable of smacking a baseball off the tall batting tee, they can catch flies and field ground balls. Or they're playing Wiffle ball or stickball, both of which are rooted in baseball skills.

By the time they're 11 and 12 (the ages of the youngsters featured in this book), many have had as much as five or six years of baseball experience, and they're highly skilled. They can snag a line drive, execute a double play, hit the cutoff man, drag bunt, or go with the pitch.

Television is one reason for their polish. "I watch a baseball game on television for the enjoyment I get out of it," says Tom Mineo, assistant coach of the East Longmeadow (Massachusetts) Cardinals. "Not my son [11-year-old Tom, Jr.]. He has a different reason. He'll sit down and watch nine innings of a

Yankee game just for the tips and tricks he picks up. His batting stance is Don Mattingly's. And for a while, he was using Rickey Henderson's snatch catch in the outfield. The other kids do the same. They imitate their heroes."

Besides what they get from television, baseball-minded kids learn about the sport from the coaches of the teams they play for. They also learn from the baseball clinics and schools they attend, from the instruction books they read and the instruction videos they watch. They learn from baseball cards, which almost all of them collect.

In *Baseball Kids,* talented youngsters speak out on baseball, discussing much of what they know and feel about baseball. In so doing, they disclose the special skills and knowledge required to be successful in the sport.

MIKE ST. CLAIR

Pitcher
Shortstop

A pitcher for four years, Mike St. Clair has thrown many one-hitters and no-hitters.

As any coach will tell you, the key to throwing a fastball is good arm speed. The faster your arm moves forward as you deliver the pitch, the faster the ball will travel.

But to get that arm speed, you must push hard off your back foot as you stride toward home plate. Not only does a strong leg push increase your arm speed, it takes some of the strain off your arm.

Fast arm speed and a strong leg push are qualities displayed

Name: **Michael St. Clair**
Nickname: **Mike**
Age: **12**
Height: **5′ 3 1/2″** Weight: **135**
Bats: **Right** Throws: **Right**
Team: **Cardinals; East Longmeadow, Massachusetts**
Position: **Pitcher, Shortstop**
Other Sports: **Golf, Basketball, Soccer, Hockey**
Favorite Uniform Number: **8**
Favorite Big League Team: **Boston Red Sox**
Favorite TV Program: **"The Wonder Years"**
Hobbies: **Collecting baseball cards**

by right-hander Mike St. Clair, who approaches baseball with both skill and intelligence. His coach calls him "very knowledgeable" about the game. While he is serious-minded, he never fails to enjoy the game. "He likes to play," says his coach.

Mike began in baseball at a very early age, at three. That's how old he was when his dad started teaching him how to hit and catch. They used a Wiffle ball and a plastic bat. By the time Mike was five, he and his dad had moved up to a regulation baseball and small wooden bat.

At six, Mike started playing tee ball. Usually the team's shortstop, Mike played tee ball for two years.

Mike still plays some shortstop but pitching is what he focuses on nowadays. "I like pitching because it really gets you into the game," he says. "You get psyched up.

"And I like it because it puts you one-on-one with the batter. There's always that challenge; either you win or lose."

Mike's favorite big league pitcher is Roger Clemens of the Boston Red Sox. He's followed Clemens's career for a long time,

Pitching "really gets you into the game," Mike says. "You get psyched up."

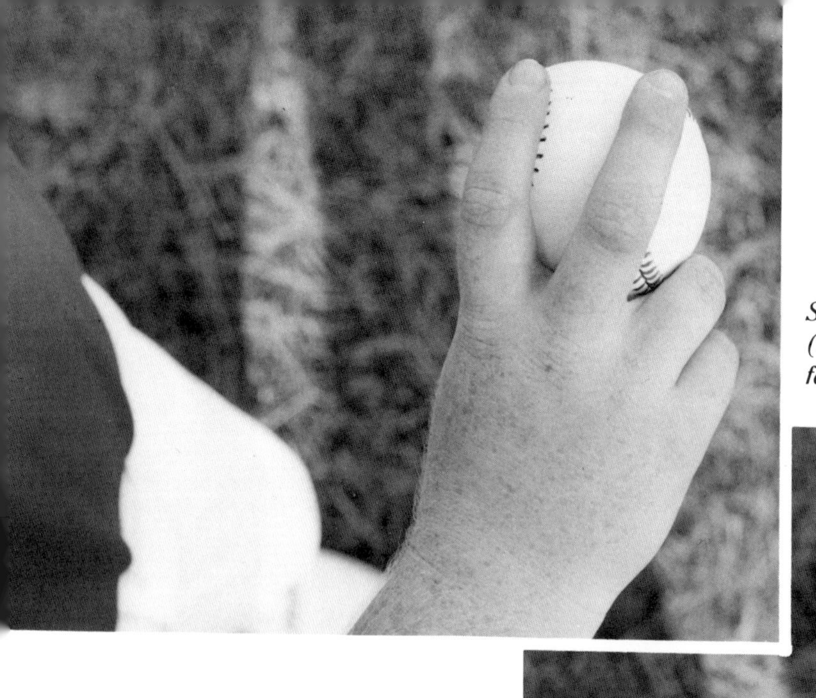

St. Clair's two-seam fastball (left) and four-seam fastball.

Mike St. Clair calls his change-up an "OK change."

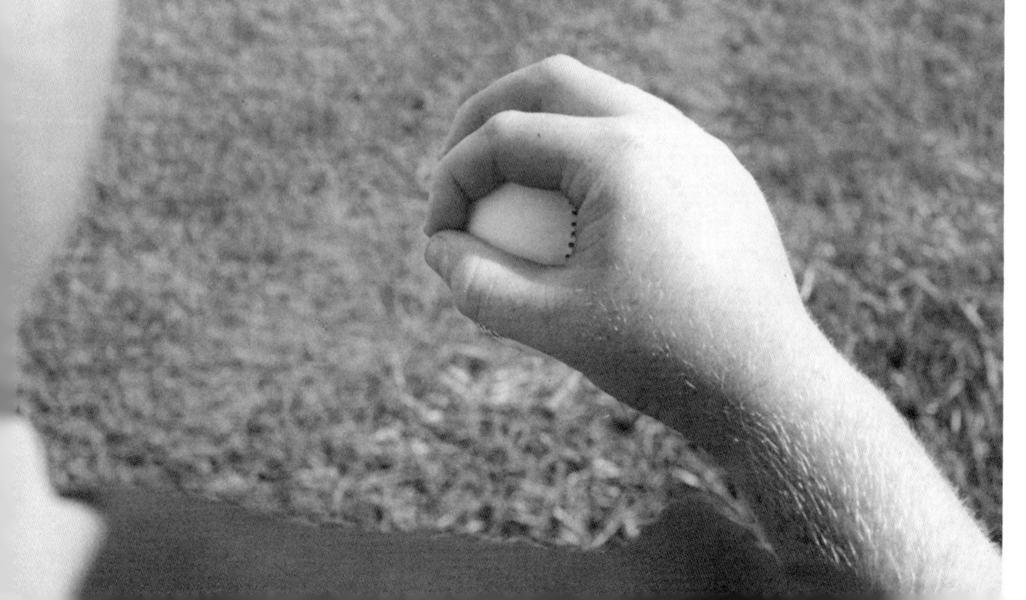

ever since Clemens was a college player at the University of Texas. "He's got a perfect motion," says Mike. "When he begins his windup, for example, he puts the ball in his glove, and he extends the glove out in front of his body. Then, with the ball still deep in his glove, he takes his grip with his right hand. The batter can't see the kind of grip he's taking, whether he's going to throw a curve, a slider, or whatever."

Any difficulties that Mike has had as a pitcher have been more emotional than physical. "One of the biggest problems I used to have was getting upset when things weren't going right," he says. "I used to get mad at myself when I'd walk a batter or two. I had to learn to overcome this because it was hurting me out there, hurting my control."

Mike's dad helped him. Says Mike: "He told me to realize that even the best pitchers walk batters and give up hits, and even the best hitters strike out. So when these things happen to me, I shouldn't get upset. You can't do anything about it."

Mike's advice to young pitchers goes back to that experience. "Never get down on yourself," he says. "That's the biggest thing. When you get down on yourself, you can't pitch."

Mike keeps to the right side of the rubber when he starts his windup. His ball travels on a diagonal, from right to left, and breaks right over the plate. "If I were to pitch from the middle of the rubber, as many pitchers do, the ball would break outside to a right-handed hitter. As it is now, with the ball kind of angling in, the batter is more likely to let it go by for a called strike, or swing and foul it off."

Mike explained the grips he uses. "If I'm throwing a fastball, I'll sometimes use a four-seam grip. It makes the ball spin forward and then back. It also makes the ball look smaller to the hitter. The four-seam fastball is very hard to hit.

"Or I'll grip it on just two seams and put a nice spin on it. The ball will sink a little. Sometimes it tails away. It's hard to hit solidly."

Mike's change-up pitch is what he calls an "OK change." "My grip on the ball is like the OK sign you give with your thumb and fingers. The tips of my thumb and forefinger touch to form an O, while the other three fingers are spread apart."

Mike has been working with the same catcher, Alan Hubbard, since he was seven years old. Alan often comes over to Mike's house and they practice together.

"Because we've been working together for so long," says Mike, "he knows how I like to pitch, where I want to put the ball. He knows when I want to throw a certain pitch. And he can tell when I throw a few bad pitches. When that happens, he'll come out to the plate and say something like, 'Just relax. Take it easy. Just play ball with the catcher.' "

With Mike's pitching experience, he has learned to size up batters. "When there is a power hitter at the plate, I like to throw the first pitch on the outside corner, and the second pitch on the inside corner. You can't let the ball get close to the middle of the plate because that's where they like it. Then, if it's 0 and 2, I like to waste a pitch, maybe throw it high and inside or low and outside.

"On the next pitch, with the count 1 and 2, I'll probably take the safe way out again, and not give him a pitch to hit, maybe go low and outside again. Or I might come inside and try to get him to hit a ground ball. Or maybe I'll throw a change-up, which can throw off his timing. He'll swing earlier—and maybe miss. Or he'll hesitate or hit off his front foot, and not get a solid hit."

Mike feels that being a pitcher has helped him as a hitter. "When I'm at bat, I sometimes can figure out what the pitcher is going to do. I know the first pitch is going to be a strike. That's what most pitchers do—try for a strike on the first pitch. I also know when to expect certain pitches. When the count is 0 and 2, I look for a change-up."

Being a pitcher helps Mike see mistakes that batters make. "They swing at pitches that are out of the strike zone, especially high pitches. I don't know exactly why they do this; maybe it's because they're too anxious to swing. Another mistake they make is not swinging level; they swing up at the pitch. When a batter swings up, most times he'll foul off the ball."

PAT CAMPBELL

Left Field
Third Base

A contact hitter, Pat Campbell has a smooth, compact swing.

Solid in the field and a determined hitter with a fluid swing, Pat Campbell became an outfielder almost by accident. Several years ago, when he showed up to play tee ball for the first time, he thought he might like to play an infield position. Since they were all filled, Pat was sent to the outfield. He wasn't too happy about it then but it's worked out well for him. "I like the outfield now," he says.

Earlier in his career, Pat also did some pitching but he hasn't

Name: **Pat Campbell**
Nickname: **Soupy**
Age: **11**
Height: **5′** Weight: **85**
Bats: **Right** Throws: **Right**
Team: **Cardinals; East Longmeadow, Massachusetts**
Position: **Left Field, Third Base**
Other Sports: **Football, Soccer**
Favorite Uniform Number: **7**
Favorite Big League Team: **New York Yankees**
Favorite TV Program: **"The Cosby Show"**
Hobbies: **Cartooning, Collecting baseball cards**

tried that recently. "Our team has plenty of pitchers," he says, "and they're all faster and more accurate than I am."

When Pat first started playing baseball, he was a little bit fearful at the plate. He had a tendency to back away on inside pitches. "Toward the end of each season in tee ball," he recalls, "the coaches would pitch underhand to us to give us some experience facing a pitcher. But that was nothing like going up against a fastball pitcher."

Pat's brother, Jason, who is several years older than Pat, helped him overcome his fear. The two would go to a local park where a batting cage was available, and Jason would pitch to Pat. "He pitched pretty fast," Pat says. "He used to play in the league I play in now, so he knew what normal pitching speed was. And he pitched from a normal distance. He helped me a lot."

Recently, another problem developed, one that was causing Pat to strike out frequently. As he swung, Pat was moving his head. His teammates told him he was "taking his head out." Pat's dad told him the same thing. "Keep your eyes on the ball," he said. Once Pat learned to keep his head still, he cut down on his number of strikeouts.

During summer vacation, Pat plays baseball almost every day. If he doesn't have a league game scheduled, he plays hardball at a local park with his friends. They also play Wiffle ball and a baseball-type game with a tennis ball. There are only a few kids on each team—a pitcher and a couple of infielder-outfielders.

Pat likes everything there is to like about baseball—hitting, running the bases, and chasing down fly balls. He likes being with his friends. About the only thing he doesn't like is when he's not chosen to start a game and has to spend a couple of innings on the bench. "It happens quite a lot," he says, "and it's no fun."

His coach admires Pat because he's so adaptable. "Anywhere you ask him to play, he'll play," says the coach, "or at least give it a try."

Pat has worked hard on his hitting. He admires Don Mattingly of the New York Yankees, though he doesn't try to imitate him completely. He knows he has to develop his own way of swinging.

"When I take my stance, I'm a little bit pigeon-toed; my feet turn inward. This makes it easier for me to pivot when I swing, which gives me more power. It also makes it easier for me to take a stride [toward the pitcher] with my left foot as I swing. Don Mattingly toes in when he takes his batting stance. But I don't crouch down the way Mattingly does. I stand straighter.

"I normally hit the ball toward shortstop, toward left center field. With an outside pitch, I'll try to pull the ball. But when I'm up against a really fast pitcher and I can't get around on the ball, I'll probably end up going to right field. But if I can get the bat around, I'll go to left field with it."

Going to baseball camp helped Pat a lot. "I learned how to drag bunt—how to push the ball down the first or third base lines and actually be running at the time the bat meets the ball.

"I also learned how to hit inside pitches. We had a drill that taught me how to do it. You stand fairly close to a fence, maybe only two or three feet from it, and then swing the bat hard over and over again, being careful not to hit the fence with the bat end. You have to tuck in your arms to be able to do it, the way you do when you swing at an inside pitch. It feels awkward at first, but when you keep doing it you get used to it. I can really drill pitches on the inside now."

Pat is skilled and experienced as an outfielder. "You always have to know exactly where you're going to throw the ball when

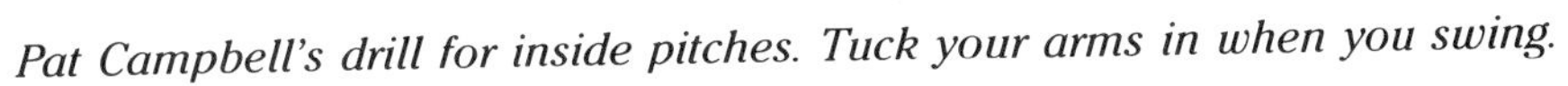

Pat Campbell's drill for inside pitches. Tuck your arms in when you swing.

it's hit to you. If there's a runner on second with one out or no outs, and you catch a fly, you have to realize that he might be going to try to tag up and score, so you have to get the ball to third base in a hurry. If it's the same situation and a line-drive base hit comes to you, it's a good idea to run the ball in toward the infield. If you throw it, the runner might go all the way home."

Pat adjusts his position, depending on which batter comes to the plate. "I know most of the batters in our league, their hitting styles. When a good hitter comes to bat, I move back a little, and toward the infield for weak hitters."

Pat knows that on fly balls, the first thing to do is get right in front of the ball. And he always uses two hands to catch flies. "If the ball is below my waist, I keep the palm turned up and the fingers together. On balls that are up around my face, I keep the back of the glove toward my face with my thumbs together."

When a fly ball comes in between Pat in left field and the center fielder, they decide who is going after it. If the center fielder yells, "I've got it!" then Pat lets him take it and backs him up. "But if I think it's my ball, I'll do the yelling and make the catch, and then he backs me up. We always back each other up. If a line drive gets past me, the center fielder is there to make the play. I don't have to turn and chase it.

"Most of our games are played on fields that have fences in the outfield, so I've had to learn to be careful when going back for any ball that goes deep. I sometimes go all the way back to the fence and then come in to make the catch."

Pat goes to baseball camp in the summer. "That's helped to make me a better fielder. I learned not to backpedal. The coach taught me to turn, turn to my left, and run back, watching the ball as I go. You move faster; you cover lots more ground."

Throwing is the biggest problem Pat has. He used to throw

To get a fly ball that's hit deep, don't backpedal; turn and run back.

sidearm, but is able to throw farther overhand. "But when I try to throw the ball hard, I sometimes throw it too high and it goes over the cutoff man's head. I'd like to be able to throw the ball low and hard, and so that it arrives on one skip bounce. In tag-up situations with a runner on third, I don't try to throw the ball all the way to home plate.

"I spent most of last summer practicing by throwing the ball into a net from which it would rebound. I'd catch and throw it again. This not only helped my throwing, but I could practice my catching, too.

"When I want to practice catching pop flies, I stand about 15 or 20 feet away from the net, and I throw the ball so it strikes the net near the bottom. Then it rebounds high into the air. I get a little closer when I want to practice fielding one-bounce line drives. And then I aim more toward the top of the net when I throw."

OMAR RAMIREZ

Second Base
Third Base
Pitcher

Omar's ambition is to play baseball as a professional.

When Omar Ramirez was about six years old, and his family lived in the South Bronx, which is part of New York City, all the kids in the neighborhood played baseball. They played in the streets using a plastic bat and a blue rubber ball. Omar wanted to play, too, but the older kids told him he wasn't good enough. He was as he recalls, one of the "scrubbiest" of players.

Omar's cousin, Michael Vartas, and an uncle helped him to improve. Michael, a pitcher, had been a high school and college

Name: **Omar Ramirez**
Nickname: **(none)**
Age: **13**
Height: **5′ 3″** Weight: **110**
Bats: **Right and Left** Throws: **Right**
Team: **Gladiators; Bronx, New York**
Position: **Second Base, Third Base, Pitcher**
Other Sports: **Football**
Favorite Uniform Number: **8**
Favorite Big League Team: **New York Mets, Montreal Expos**
Favorite TV Program: **"This Week in Baseball"**
Hobbies: **Collecting baseball cards, Playing Nintendo video games**

player. Omar's uncle would take him to an empty lot to practice. On the wall of a building that faced the lot, a strike-box—a square about 12 inches on each side with an X in the center—had been painted. The strike-box serves somewhat the same purpose as a home plate. A pitched ball that hits within the square is a strike. One that doesn't is a ball.

Omar would stand in front of the strike-box, bat in hand, and his cousin, would pitch to him. Omar would try to smack the ball over a gate on the side of the lot opposite him. Anytime he did, Michael would reward him with a dollar bill. At first, they used a rubber ball but after a year or so advanced to a hardball.

Omar appears fearless at the plate today but he admits being somewhat afraid of pitched balls when he was a "little kid." He had a habit of backing out of the batter's box on inside pitches. Michael cured Omar of that. Whenever a pitch went inside and Omar started to back away, Michael ordered him to "Stay there!" If Omar moved, Michael threatened to hit him with the ball. Since Omar did not want to get smacked in the ribs with a baseball, he learned to "stay there." Today, Omar says he has no fears at the plate. He backs away only when a pitch heads right for him.

Omar's cousin also worked with Omar on his fielding. He hit ground balls to Omar, and he hit them real hard, harder than Omar ever saw in competition. He hit them so hard that later, when Omar played an infield position in a game and a ground ball came to him, it always seemed to be softly hit.

As Omar kept practicing with his two relatives, he kept getting better. When his family moved to another section of the Bronx, Omar joined two hardball leagues. In one of them, he was named to the league's All-Star team two years in a row.

Omar practices almost every day. There's a strike-box on the wall of a building across the street from where he lives, and he and his friends meet there. They use a plastic bat and a rubber ball in their games. Omar also practices hardball twice a week.

Omar's ambition is to play a pro sport as a professional. Baseball is the one on which he plans to concentrate. Although he's just begun junior high school, he's already planning to play baseball in high school and college. Omar also plays football on an amateur team in the Bronx. He's a wide receiver. But when he goes on to high school, he plans to drop football. "I can't play both sports," he says. "I'd be exhausted."

Omar, who hits both right-handed and left-handed, has this to say about hitting:

"I'm a natural right-handed hitter but I taught myself to hit leftie. It was something I wanted to be able to do. I learned to hit left-handed by practicing from that side with a Wiffle ball and a plastic bat. I practiced almost everyday. It took me about two months to learn. Now I always bat left-handed when a right-handed pitcher is pitching, and I'm pretty good at it. I know my

A natural right-handed batter, Omar taught himself also to hit left-handed.

batting average against right-handers is higher than it would be if I had to hit rightie against them. I also hit left-handed whenever I go to the plate to sacrifice bunt. It's a big advantage in getting down to first base."

Howard Johnson, the third baseman for the New York Mets, is Omar's favorite player. "I like him because he's both a contact hitter and a long-ball hitter—like I am. But I don't copy Johnson and his batting style. I use my own. I bat the way I want, the way I feel comfortable."

Omar uses an open stance, with his front foot a little bit farther from home plate than his back foot. "This makes it easier for me to pull the ball, which I usually like to do. I choke-up on the bat when I'm going to pull. But if I'm going the other way, to right field when I'm hitting rightie, then I grip down at the end."

His cousin got him to keep his right elbow up when he hits. "This helps to give you a level swing, which is very important. A level swing is a powerful swing.

"I take a short stride toward the pitcher—it's only about four inches—with my front foot as I swing. I watch the ball from the time it leaves the pitcher's hand almost until it hits the bat.

"I always take the first pitch. If it's a ball, you know the pitcher has to come in with the next pitch. You know that pitch has to be good. I get ready to hit it."

Omar plays both second base and shortstop for his team. The fields they play on usually have rocks on the ground. "You have to be careful about charging hard-hit ground balls," he says. "At the last second, the ball can take a bad hop. You can only charge slow grounders.

"When you do go to field a ground ball, get down low. Put your glove on the ground. Always get in front of the ball. Block it with your body. Even if it hits you in the chest, it won't hurt you. I

When he wants to pull the ball, Omar chokes-up on the bat.

used to try to field the ball by reaching out to one side for it. I made a lot of errors doing that. Now I get in front of the ball, and last year I made only one error."

Omar Ramirez has some other fielding tips. "Take your time with your throws. From second, you don't have to throw far. It's not like at third. There's no need to hurry.

"When I'm playing third, I charge in to field bunts that are hit to the right side of the infield. The catcher tells me where to throw, to first base or second base. When I'm playing second base, the first baseman charges in, and I cover first."

PAT HELLYER

Second Base Catcher

When rounding second or third, touch the inside of the base as you go by.

At 4-foot-6, 75 pounds, Pat Hellyer, who often catches, is one of the smaller members of his team. He is also one of the most valued. In fact, when it comes to base-running and bunting, Pat has no equal.

Pat is admired as a gutsy player, too. "When he gets in there to catch, he's a real competitor," says his coach. "He'll stand up to any six-footer who wants to run him down."

His coach also praises Pat because he's so knowledgeable

Name: **Patrick Hellyer**
Nickname: **Pat**
Age: **11**
Height: **4′ 6″** Weight: **75**
Bats: **Right and Left** Throws: **Right**
Team: **Cardinals; East Longmeadow, Massachusetts**
Position: **Second Base, Catcher**
Other Sports: **Soccer, Basketball**
Favorite Uniform Number: **12**
Favorite Big League Team: **Boston Red Sox**
Favorite TV Program: **"Great Unsolved Mysteries"**
Hobbies: **Wiffle ball**

about the game. "And he pays attention out there," says the coach. "He knows what he's supposed to be doing."

Pat sharpened his skills by attending baseball camp for several weeks during two different summers. The camp was held on the campus of Springfield [Massachusetts] College. College coaches did the instructing. About 200 youngsters attended the camp each year.

"They had a lot of clinics at the camp," Pat recalls, "on hitting, fielding, playing the outfield, catching, bunting, base-running—different things. You could go to whatever clinics you wanted." Pat specialized in bunting and base-running.

How many bases does Pat usually steal in a game? It depends on how many times he gets on base. "If I get on with singles," he says, "I'll steal two bases, maybe even three." In one recent season, Pat stole home four times.

"Lean forward as you run," is the advice Pat gives anyone wanting to become a speedster. "Try to run on your toes. Pump your arms."

Pat also puts his running to good use in other sports he plays, particularly soccer and tennis. When he gets to high school, he looks forward to becoming a member of the track team. And if his success in the past is any guide to the future, you can probably look for Pat in the 1996 Olympic Games.

Like any good base runner, Pat knows that you never take a lead unless you know exactly where the ball is. He watches out for the hidden-ball trick. "That's when you're on first base, say, and you're watching the pitcher, who looks like he's beginning his delivery. You step off the base. Then the first baseman, who has the ball hidden in his glove, suddenly tags you.

"Earlier this season, our first baseman and pitcher worked the hidden-ball trick. But, at just about the same time the first baseman was tagging the runner, our pitcher forgot and stepped onto the rubber. So the pitcher was called for a balk and the runner wasn't called out."

Pat has some tips about running the bases. Speed is important, but how and where you touch the base can make a difference. "When I hit a ground ball to the infield," he says, "I try to run right through first base, touching the front of the base as I go by. Jumping for the base or sliding into it slows you down. On a pop-up to the shortstop or second baseman, I do the same thing—run hard for first base."

On ground balls or fly balls hit to the outfield, Pat has a different tactic. "About halfway down the base line, I start curving to my right and then curve back, so I can make a wide turn at first. I touch the inside of the base, check where the ball is, and decide whether I can go on to second. When I hit a fly ball into the outfield, I take the same route to first, checking to see whether the outfielder makes the catch."

The runner has to decide what to do. "When you are on first

and there is a ground ball, you run hard for second," advises Pat. "On a fly ball to the outfield, you go halfway between first and second, and watch what happens. If the ball is a hit or is dropped, you keep going. If it's caught, you get back to first fast to prevent a double play. If there's a bunt, make sure the batter has bunted the ball on the ground before heading to second. If the ball is popped up and caught, you may have to dive back into first."

Watching the coaches and listening to them pays off. If Pat is on third with one out or no outs and the batter hits a ball deep to the outfield, the third base coach will tell him to get back to the base and get ready to tag up. "I put my left foot on the base and step with my right toward home plate. I keep outside of the base line. That way, if I should happen to get hit with the batted ball, I won't be called out. The rules say if you get hit with a batted ball while you're in fair territory, you're out."

If Pat is the runner on first or second and goes back to the base, he watches the coach to see if he flashes the steal sign. If he gets the sign, he watches the pitcher carefully. "Keep evenly balanced as you take your lead," he says. "Your arms are down at your sides. You're ready to go in either direction—back to the base or to second. Once the pitcher starts his delivery, lifting his front leg, you take off. You don't look to see whether the catcher is going to make a throw. You never turn your head. You just go."

If Pat is heading for second base or third base, and the infielder has the ball in his glove, and the glove is down in front of the base, he goes in with a hook slide. "I slide right past the base, hooking it with one foot as I go by.

"Say you're hooking on the right side of the base. Begin your slide three or four feet before you reach it. Slide on your right

Pat Hellyer demonstrates a hook slide. The idea is to "hook" the base as you go by.

Pop-up slide enables you to get quickly to your feet so you can advance to the next base.

On a sacrifice bunt attempt, Pat faces the pitcher, knees bent.

side and right hip. Slide right past the base, and hook it with your left foot.

"Our team also uses the pop-up slide. With this, you finish the slide by 'popping' to your feet so you can advance to the next base. One leg is extended as you go into the base and the other is bent and beneath you. You slide straight for the base, straightening the bent leg as you go in. This, plus your momentum, brings you to your feet, so you're ready to take off for the next base."

When it comes to bunting, this is what Pat has to say:

"On our team, the third base coach gives us signs to tell us when to bunt. When trying for a sacrifice bunt, take your regular batting stance. But when the pitcher starts his delivery, step forward with your rear foot so you're facing the pitcher almost squarely.

"Hold the bat level in front of your body, sliding your top hand up the bat to about the trademark. Keep your thumb on top, your fingers underneath. The other hand, which grips tighter, controls the bat.

"Bend your knees; bend forward from the waist. When the pitch is high, you have to reach up to make contact. When it's low, bend your knees to get down. Just meet the ball with the bat. It should 'give' a little as the ball makes contact.

"If you are bunting for a hit, lay the ball down and start running at the same time."

DAN DESILETS

Left Field
Center Field
Second Base

An outfielder in baseball, Dan Desilets is a football running back and linebacker.

Versatile, dependable, and very likable, Dan Desilets has played several different infield and outfield positions for his team. If he had his choice, he'd prefer playing center field or second base. "More happens when you're in center or at second," he says. But he doesn't complain about being shifted about. "I figure the coach is using me where I can help the team the most," he says.

Dan got interested in baseball at six or seven, when his family

Name: **Daniel Desilets**
Nickname: **Dan**
Age: **11**
Height: **5′ 2 1/2″** Weight: **103**
Bats: **Right** Throws: **Right**
Team: **Cardinals; East Longmeadow, Massachusetts**
Position: **Left Field, Center Field, Second Base**
Other Sports: **Football, Basketball**
Favorite Uniform Number: **13**
Favorite Big League Team: **Boston Red Sox**
Favorite TV Program: **"Alf"**
Hobbies: **Deer hunting**

lived in Braintree in eastern Massachusetts. His dad and mom used to take him to watch Little League games in which his brother, Rob, took part.

When the Desilets family moved to East Longmeadow in the western part of the state, Dan joined a team. Baseball was valuable to him because it helped him to make friends in a community new to the family.

Last fall, Dan started playing football for the East Longmeadow Spartans. On defense, he's an outside linebacker; on offense, a left halfback. In his first football season, Dan was named the team's Most Valuable Player.

He enjoys playing football a bit more than baseball. "I like the action," he says. "I like making tackles and running with the ball. I like the hitting, the contact."

When Dan moves on to high school, he plans to keep playing both baseball and football. If he's forced to choose one or the other, baseball may lose a solid all-around player.

However, Dan always concentrates on the game he is playing.

In the outfield, he watches the batters closely and remembers them next time they are at bat. If a batter hits to the first baseman or right fielder on his first time up, Dan adjusts his position and moves right next time that batter comes to the plate.

He watches the pitcher until he releases the ball. "As the pitcher gets ready to throw, I bend my knees and lean forward with the weight on the balls of my feet. My glove is in front of me."

When it comes to a fly ball hit between Dan and the center fielder, he lets the center fielder take it. "He's in charge of the outfielders; he's in control out there. If the center fielder calls for it, he takes it. It doesn't make any difference whether he's the first to call or the second. It's always his ball if he wants it.

"We work with one another whenever we can. Suppose the center fielder is chasing a ball that's been hit in his direction, and he can't look up. I'll yell out instructions that tell him where he's to throw the ball. I'll yell One! or Two! or Three!—meaning he's to throw the ball to first, second, or third. On fly balls that aren't hit deep, we get instructions from one of the infielders."

When asked what his biggest problem was in playing the outfield, Dan replied, "Throwing." He used to throw sidearm, and didn't start throwing overhand until this year.

"I'm not *that* accurate when I throw. One reason is because I don't always grip the ball right. When you throw, you're supposed to grip the ball with your first two fingers across the seams where they're the widest apart. Well, I sometimes grip with my fingers along the seams, which doesn't help my accuracy.

"Our coaches want us to throw overhand, starting the ball from about where your back pocket is. Then you're supposed to bring it up in a circular movement, so your hand, with your arm straight, comes over your shoulder. Then you release and follow through. Your hand ends up near your left knee.

As the pitcher gets set to throw, bend your knees, lean forward.

Coaches want their players to throw overhand, not sidearm.

"You take only one step, or rather, a step and a hop, a crow hop. And you keep your eyes on your target, the cutoff man, the base, or whatever."

Dan Desilets watches other teams play and tries to spot mistakes kids make in the outfield. He thinks that the biggest problem they have is judging where the ball is going to come down. They come in too far and the ball falls in back of them, or they go back too far and the ball falls in front of them.

"I use the tree line to help me judge fly balls," says Dan. "If the ball is above the treetops, I move back. If it's below the tree line, I move in. I think some kids do the opposite. They go back on balls below the tree line and come in on balls above the trees. I think that's why they have problems."

Dan knows that kids in the outfield make the mistake of trying to catch the ball with only one hand. "Sometimes I do that. In fact, I do it so often that when someone else on the team tries to one-hand the ball, my coach yells at *me,* 'Did you teach him to do that?' I don't know why I do it so often; I just can't seem to get the other hand around."

Often kids have trouble fielding ground balls in the outfield, according to Dan. "Once in a while I'll see a player get down on one knee to block a grounder, and he has his legs spread too far apart, and the ball rolls right through them.

"Another mistake kids make is in throwing the ball after they've made the catch. They sometimes try to throw it too far. If there's a runner racing for home plate, an outfielder might try to throw the ball all the way home instead of throwing to the cutoff man. You should always throw to the cutoff man."

BRIAN KARAVISH

Third Base
First Base

When playing third base, you're always moving; you have to be fast.

A smooth-fielding third baseman, occasionally a pitcher, and his team's clean-up hitter, Brian Karavish says he likes baseball for the fun and excitement he gets from the sport. "There's always an exciting quality to the game," he says, "always an intensity."

Hitting is what Brian likes the most. "Even when you hit a slow grounder, there's fun to it," he says. "You run as hard as you can to first base, and maybe the fielder will overthrow the base and

Name: **Brian Karavish**
Nickname: **Fish**
Age: **12**
Height: **5′ 4 1/2″** Weight: **122**
Bats: **Right** Throws: **Right**
Team: **Cardinals; East Longmeadow, Massachusetts**
Position: **Third Base, First Base**
Other Sports: **Football, Hockey**
Favorite Uniform Number: **1 or 13**
Favorite Big League Team: **New York Yankees**
Favorite TV Program: **(none)**
Hobbies: **Collecting baseball cards**

you'll be safe. Or even when you strike out, there's a chance the catcher will drop the third strike, and you can race to first and beat it out."

Brian also appreciates the physical values baseball offers. "It's like aerobics," he says. "You always have to be in good shape to play it, but it's fun. You do a lot of fun things. You're not just trying to shake all the fat off of your body. It's like fun aerobics."

Now 12, Brian has been playing the game for seven or eight years, ever since his dad introduced him to a Wiffle ball and a plastic bat.

From Wiffle ball, Brian advanced to hardball. His dad would throw him grounders and fly balls, and later pitched to him.

Brian never attended any baseball camps or clinics. Outside of his dad, Brian never depended on anyone to give him advice. He says he learned hitting and fielding pretty much on his own.

He got an assist from television, however. Brian says he watches baseball on TV "all the time," and it's helped him. For example, during the first couple of years he played baseball, he had trouble striding forward with his front foot as he swung. Such a stride assures a powerful swing. Brian watched major league players on TV, and studied how they did it. He modeled his own stride after their's.

Brian works to improve his hitting by visiting a batting range a couple of times a week. The range offers robot pitchers for batters to face. You can regulate the machine to throw very fast fastballs or gentle change-ups. "I usually set the machine for 65 to 70 miles an hour," Brian says, "which is faster than most pitchers in our league pitch. This really helps me keep my bat speed up."

Brian likes playing third base because there's a lot of action there. He feels you have to be a good athlete to play the position. "You have to have good reflexes," he says. "You have to be able to move quickly to your right when the ball is pulled down the line, and you have to be able to adjust fast when the ball takes a bad hop. You have to be able to jump high in the air to pull down line drives over your head. You have to be able to throw hard and accurately.

"To someone who's thinking of becoming a third baseman, I'd tell him that one of the most important things of all is keeping alert. You always have to pay attention out there. You always have to have a good idea of where the ball is going to be going."

Brian positions himself at third base so that he always knows where the ball is going to be going. He likes to be at the edge of the outfield grass and about five feet to the left of the base. "When there's a runner on second, I move in and play about even with the bag. Then, if the runner should try to steal, I can get back to the base fast to take the throw. I also move in whenever there's a bunt situation, of course, when there's a batter at the plate who likes to bunt a lot."

Playing the same teams several times a season means getting

to know the hitters. "Sometimes you can get tipped off as to what the batter is going to do by watching his hands or feet," says Brian. "When the batter starts to square around, you know a bunt is coming. When you see a batter really step into the ball when he swings, you know he's probably a good hitter, and he's going to pull the ball or hit it far.

"Even if I've never seen a hitter before, I can tell certain things about him just by looking at him. When a big kid comes up to the plate, someone who looks like he can hit the ball hard, I play a little bit deeper and closer to the base, guarding the line. I don't want him pulling the ball into the corner for a double."

Before a game, Brian plays catch for a half hour or so with his brother, who is nine, to warm up his arm. He knows that playing third base successfully requires accurate throwing. "On throws to first, I take one step, never any more than that. And I always come over the top with the ball, that is, I throw overhand. When the ball comes to me in a double-play situation—when there's a runner on first with one out or no outs—my job is to make the fielding play, then get the ball out of my glove fast and throw to second. When I throw, I aim for the fielder's chest. If I'm accurate, he can make the catch, throw to first, and move off the base [to avoid the runner]—all in one motion."

When a batter makes a slow grounder, it's also Brian's job to make the play. If it is a dribbler, he sometimes has to cut in front of the shortstop and pick up the ball while it's still on the grassy part of the infield. "I can usually make the play bare-handed and flip underhand to first.

"On a sacrifice bunt, with a runner on first, I make the fielding play, then quickly check second base to see whether I can get the out there. If I can't, I make the throw to first base. Then I hurry back to cover third to prevent the runner from advancing."

Making the play on an attempted steal, with the ball coming in from the catcher, means a different tactic. "I straddle the bag, make the catch, and then try for a sweep tag, just touching the runner's spikes as he comes sliding in. I try to make the tag with the glove's webbing."

He can handle most batted balls, but line drives that bounce right in front of his glove can cause trouble. "Sometimes I'm afraid the ball is going to bounce off my foot or my glove and hit me in the face, so I turn away and then try to make the play blindly. When the ball goes by me or I make an error, I feel badly."

On throws to first, take one step, never any more. Throw overhand.

SENECA PEREZ

Center Field

Seneca Perez prefers playing the outfield. "I like all the running," he says.

Seneca Perez, who lives in New York City's borough of the Bronx, didn't start playing baseball for a team in an organized league until he was 12. Before that, he played stickball or Wiffle ball in the streets. And often he practiced with his stepfather in parks near where the family lived.

Seneca was about three when he first became interested in baseball. His father was a member of a local softball team and

Name: **Seneca Perez**
Nickname: **Elias**
Age: **12**
Height: **5′ 1/2″** Weight: **110**
Bats: **Right** Throws: **Right**
Team: **Gladiators; Bronx, New York**
Position: **Center Field**
Other Sports: **Football, Basketball, Track, Swimming**
Favorite Uniform Number: **4**
Favorite Big League Team: **New York Mets**
Favorite TV Program: **"This Week in Baseball"**
Hobbies: **Collecting baseball cards, Playing dominoes, Card games**

Seneca would be brought to the park to watch him play. His mother and brother, Marcus, two years younger than Seneca, attended the games, too. "There were no stands for seating," Seneca says. "You stood around in back of the bench where the players sat.

"Baseball looked like an exciting game to me," Seneca recalls. "I wanted to play it."

When Seneca got older, several times he joined teams in local leagues, but the teams never got to play. One time the coach abruptly abandoned the team, and it broke up. "It was too bad," Seneca says. "There were a lot of kids that wanted to play."

Meanwhile, Seneca was learning about baseball from his stepfather. He would take Seneca to a local park afternoons after school, on weekends, and during summer vacations. "We used a softball and wooden bat," Seneca says. "He pitched underhand to me at first. After I learned to hit, he pitched overhand."

Seneca says that one reason he likes baseball is because the game can be played in so many ways. Playing second is different from being the team's catcher. Pitching is different from playing the outfield. "There are many different things you have to know and learn," he says.

Seneca likes playing the outfield the best. "I like moving around, running," he says. "You have to do a lot of that in the outfield. You have to move in to get ground balls and pop-ups. You have to run back for long flies. I like all that running."

And Seneca also likes playing the outfield for the opportunities it gives him to display his skills. He says: "Suppose a guy gets a base hit, and then tries to go to second, take an extra base. I like to throw him out from deep in the outfield. I like to show what kind of an arm I have.

"It's the same when there're runners on second and third with one out or no outs, and the batter hits a fly ball to me in center field. The runner on third tags up and tries to score. It's up to me to try to throw him out at home. I like to do that—and I have done it. I like to show off a little bit."

Seneca's favorite major league player, a center fielder like himself, is the dazzling Willie Mays, perhaps the best center fielder in major league history. In addition to the exceptional defensive skills he displayed, Mays was one of the standout sluggers of his day. He batted over .300 ten times and smacked 660 home runs in 22 seasons, which puts him third on the all-time list behind Hank Aaron (755) and Babe Ruth (714).

Mays's final season in baseball was 1974, which was before Seneca was born. How does Seneca happen to know about Mays and his achievements? He first heard about Mays from a videotape about the New York Mets that his stepfather brought home. In it, Mays is featured as one of the New York team's all-time greats. Later, Seneca happened to spot Mays's autobiography, titled *Say Hey,* in a bookstore window. He told his mother about the book and she bought it for him as a birthday gift.

Seneca admires Mays not only for his accomplishments as a hitter and fielder but also for the role he played in helping to integrate baseball. Mays joined the New York Giants in 1951, only four years after Jackie Robinson had become the first black to play in the major leagues.

Another of Seneca's favorite players is Lenny Dykstra, who played center field for the Mets until he was traded to the Philadelphia Phillies in 1989. "Remember how Dykstra used to make diving catches in the outfield?" Seneca asks. "Sometimes he didn't have to do that. He could have caught the ball without diving. I liked that. Sometimes I try to do the same thing." It saddened Seneca when the Mets dealt Dykstra to the Phils.

Seneca is a contact hitter; he goes up to the plate with the idea of getting on base, not to hit a home run. Here's what he has to say about hitting:

"When you go up to the plate, the first thing to do is get comfortable. Spread your feet. Keep your elbows up. Always keep your eyes on the ball.

"When you swing, keep your head still. Watch the ball. If you move your head, you won't hit anything.

"Always bend your knees. Bending your knees helps to give you a more powerful swing.

"Sometimes I choke-up on the bat; sometimes I grip it at the end. It depends. If I'm facing a pitcher who likes to come inside with the ball, then I choke-up half an inch or so. When I choke-up, it's easier for me to get the bat around to hit a pitch that's inside.

"When I'm up against a pitcher who throws outside I take my

When hitting, "Keep your elbows up," says Seneca. "Keep your eyes on the ball."

regular grip, gripping down at the end. Then it's easier for me to reach out and get balls that are outside."

When Seneca first started playing for the Gladiators, he was the lead-off hitter. The coach gave him signs telling him whether to swing or take the pitch. "I always had to take the first pitch.

But when I got to know the pitchers, know what kind of pitches they threw, I became a better hitter, and then the coach let me make up my own mind whether to swing or take."

His stepfather's advice was, "Wait for your pitch and swing," and that's what he does. "I watch the pitch. If it looks like it's going to be a strike and it's a pitch I like, I swing."

Seneca knows that curve balls in his league are not real curve balls. But they can be a problem. "What a kid may do is throw a fastball with a sidearm delivery. The ball looks like it's going to hit you and then it slides over the plate. This kind of pitch I don't like. It gives me trouble."

In his first year with the Gladiators, playing the outfield was no picnic for Seneca. He discusses some of his difficulties.

"When I first started playing the outfield, one of my problems was that I didn't move fast enough on fly balls. I used to wait and see when the ball was going to come down before I started running for it. I was a late starter. By the time I got to the ball, all I could do was pick it up. My coach kept telling me I had to run sooner.

"I practiced in the park. I had someone hit fly balls to me, and I learned to start for the ball as soon as it left the bat. I learned to be there when the ball came down."

On ground balls, Seneca fields the ball like an infielder, getting in front of the ball, bending low, putting his glove on the ground. When the ball is hit hard, he gets down on one knee to block it. "The only problem I have with ground balls is when the outfield is messed up, has holes in it. Then the ball can hit a hole and bounce over your shoulder. About all you can do is try to field the ball before it reaches the hole."

He used to have trouble when a fly ball was hit in between him and one of the other outfielders. "When that happens, the center fielder is supposed to take the ball. But he's also supposed to call

When making throws from the outfield, Perez grips the ball with his fingers over the seams at their widest point.

To strengthen his arm, Seneca practices throwing frequently.

for it. I didn't always do that. From practicing with my stepfather in the park, I was used to just running and catching the ball. I didn't have to worry about any other outfielders. I never had to call for a ball."

When he started playing in a league there were almost some bad collisions. "Once, the left fielder and I started to go for the same ball and we didn't see one another, and no one called. Just before we crashed, I spotted him. When I tried to stop, I went down. I slid because the grass was wet. We didn't run into each other but we didn't catch the ball either. It just dropped. I picked it up and threw it to second, holding the guy to a single.

"Since then, I've gotten better about calling for the ball. I don't have problems like that anymore."

Seneca practices throwing a lot. His mother's cousin has a videotape with instructions about how to play baseball. One thing it shows is how to grip the ball to throw it—across the seams where they're widest apart with your first two fingers, your thumb underneath. "I always try to throw the ball like that," says Seneca.

"I go to the park with my stepfather and brother almost every Saturday to practice throwing. We get far apart and then start throwing the ball to one another. My stepfather always wants to throw hard, throw with power. I try not to hang the ball in the air; I try to throw on a line. I go straight at his chest with it."

TOM MINEO

First Base
Pitcher

A contact hitter, Tom Mineo plays first base and pitches.

Tom Mineo, with three years of baseball experience, is one of the standout hitters on his team. He bats fifth. He's averaged as high as .400.

At one time, Tom swung hard, always trying for an extra-base hit. Now he's more of a contact hitter. He simply tries to hit safely. If he happens to get a double, triple, or home run, that's great, but a single is all he's trying for.

Being a contact hitter has paid dividends. His batting average

Name: **Thomas Mineo**
Nickname: **Tom**
Age: **11**
Height: **4′ 11″** Weight: **95**
Bats: **Right** Throws: **Right**
Team: **Cardinals; East Longmeadow, Massachusetts**
Position: **First Base, Pitcher**
Other Sports: **Soccer, Hockey, Basketball**
Favorite Uniform Number: **10**
Favorite Big League Team: **New York Yankees**
Favorite TV Program: **"Family Ties"**
Hobbies: **Fishing; Building car models; Collecting baseball cards, football cards, rocks, stamps, and coins**

has zoomed upward. "And I don't strike out very much," he says. "One season I struck out only once."

Tom is relaxed and confident whether at bat or in the field. You can tell he enjoys the game. One coach, in fact, describes him as carefree and happy-go-lucky. But that wasn't always the case. "The first year or so I played," he recalls, "I didn't like baseball that much. Maybe that's because I wasn't very good. But as I kept playing, I started getting better. I got better as a fielder; I got better as a hitter. And that's when baseball started being fun."

Tom looks forward to playing baseball in high school and then in college. "I'd like to play major league baseball one day," he says. His teammates and coaches agree that Tom is off to a fast start.

In his first year playing baseball, there were a few problems, though. "I was kind of afraid at the plate in my first few games. On fastballs, I was backing out of the batter's box. Then I got a hit and I was fine. When I found out I could hit the ball, I stopped being afraid. The chances of getting hit by a pitch are maybe one out of a hundred. If I think the ball is coming toward me, I just back out of the way."

Tom used to wear a batting glove to help improve his grip. He doesn't anymore. "I'm superstitious about it. At the beginning of the season, I was getting a lot of hits. Then I went into a slump. I stopped wearing the glove and started hitting again. So I haven't put it back on. Besides, the bat I've been using has pine tar on it. That works just as well as a glove."

Tom Mineo uses an open stance. "I bat kind of like Don Mattingly. I watch him on television. He has an open stance, too. The toe of my left foot is on the same line as the heel of my right foot. And I point the toes of the left foot a bit toward first base. If I don't use an open stance, I always hit to right field. That causes problems for me. I'm not the fastest runner in the world. All the right fielder has to do is throw to first and he can get me out. That actually happened to me once. The right fielder picked up the ball and threw me out at first."

As a hitter, Tom follows the advice of coaches because he knows it works. "I look right at the ball as it comes toward me. When I swing, I always step into the pitch. I like to make contact out in front of the plate so I can pull the ball. And I always try to get the barrel of the bat on the ball.

"Sometimes I'm too anxious up there. I swing at the first ball whether or not it's over the plate. Once I did that and hit a home run. But my dad says I shouldn't be so anxious, and I usually try to wait for the first good pitch."

A ball thrown over the outside corner causes him trouble. "I hate that pitch. If there are no strikes on me or only one strike, I'll let the pitch go by; I won't swing at it. If there are two strikes

Mineo has an open stance, grips the bat at the end.

on me, I'll swing. But I'm not very successful. Every time I've ever struck out, it's been on that pitch.

"Some people tell me I should stand closer to the plate, and then I'd be better able to handle pitches to the outside. But it's not that simple. I like pitches on the inside corner; that's where I get most of my power. When I move closer to the plate, the pitchers jam me, and I can't get the barrel of the bat on the ball."

Tom has played several different positions. Earlier in his career, he played third base and the outfield. Nowadays he either pitches or plays first base. Pitching is what he prefers. "I started pitching two or three years ago," he says. "I really like it. I like all the action."

He used to pitch sidearm, but that was a big problem for him. "I didn't have good control. The ball would go all over the place. So I started pitching more overhand. My dad and Jack Sullivan, a coach, helped me.

"My dad practiced with me. He caught when I pitched, and he gave me tips. One thing he did was help me with my stance. When I was beginning my windup, I was facing toward third base; that's wrong. My dad got me to change so I was facing the batter, with my right foot over the front edge of the pitching rubber. From that position, I swing my arms up and back, and pivot off my left foot."

Changing to an overhand delivery hurt his fielding for a while. "When I threw sidearm, my left leg would automatically come over into a ready position, which made it easy to field the ball. But when I changed to the overhand delivery, I was off-balance when I followed through; I was leaning toward the left. Any ground ball hit to my right was tough to field. I had to keep working on my delivery until I was comfortably balanced as I followed through, and able to move in either direction to field the ball.

Once a sidearmer, Tom now throws overhand.

"I'm pretty good when it comes to fielding my position now. Watching baseball on television helped me. When a major league player makes a fielding play, he always gets in front of the ball. And if the pitcher or any player making a play in the field happens to bobble the ball, he'll still try to get the runner at first. I do these things now."

Backing up on the bases is part of a pitcher's job—at third base or sometimes at home plate—in case there's an overthrow and the runner can advance. "When I first started pitching, I didn't know where or when I was supposed to back up," says Tom. "I had to be reminded to do it. Now I know what I'm supposed to do."

If a pitcher doesn't know the hitters, the batting order can be a tip-off as to how good they are. "When the No. 3 hitter or the clean-up hitter comes up to the plate, I know I have to bear down," says Tom. "I have to try to throw faster. I know they're among the best hitters on the team."

The catcher decides which pitch to use and gives him a target. The catcher makes up his mind when watching the batter take his practice swings. If the batter is standing away from the plate and can't reach the outside corner with his bat, the catcher will call for an outside pitch. If the batter is standing close, then he gives a target for an inside pitch to try to jam him. If he's in the middle of the batter's box, then he'll ask for a pitch down the middle.

"Sometimes I get a little wild," admits Tom. "It can be because I'm trying to aim the ball instead of just pitching naturally. Or it can happen because I get upset.

"When I have control trouble, my catcher and my coach come to the mound, and they try to calm me down. They tell me to just put the ball over the plate, to let the batter hit it, because I've got my fielders behind me."

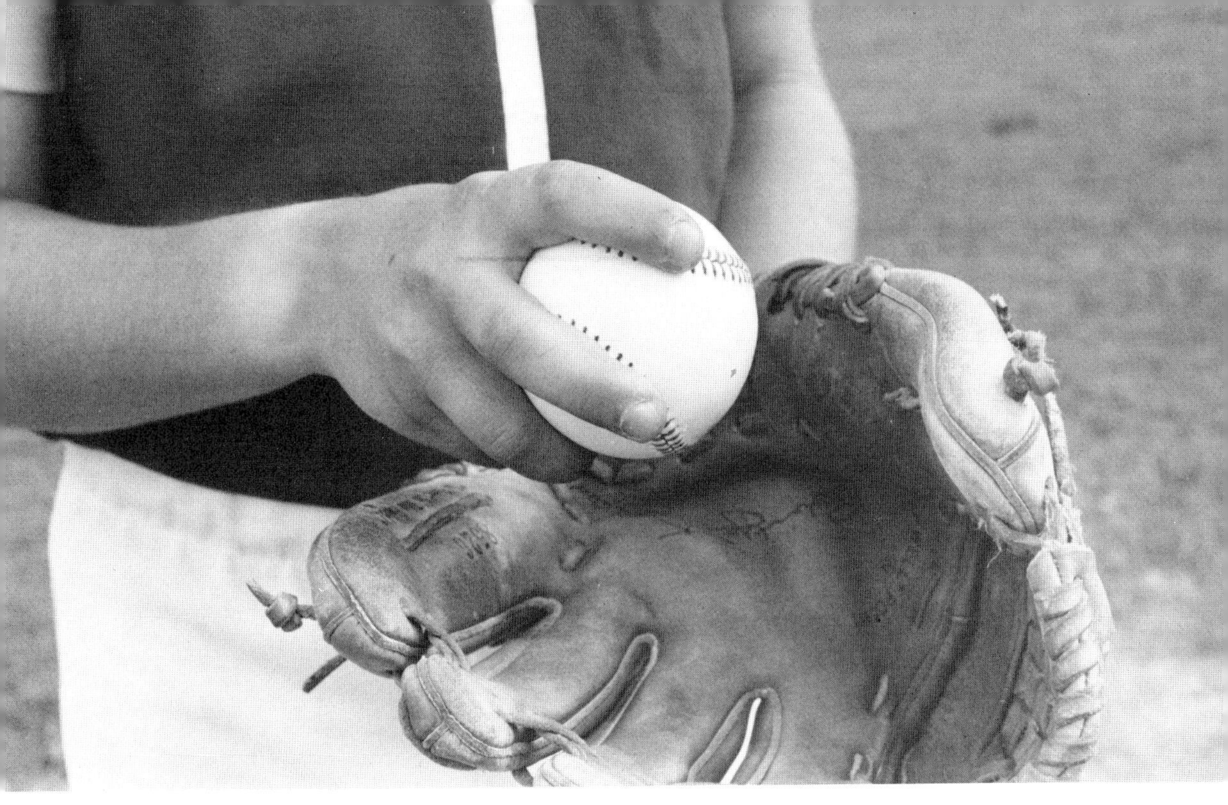

Tom Mineo shows his fastball grip (above) and his split-finger, gripped where the seams are closest together.

When he is pitching, Tom Mineo mostly throws a fastball or a change-up. "Sometimes I try to throw a curve, which doesn't always work too well. It goes too slow. I don't use it anymore. The coach doesn't like me to throw it. Neither does my dad. He says I can hurt my arm with it, and I guess he's right." For a change-up, Tom doesn't put his fingers on any of the seams and tries to throw the ball slower. With his fingers across the seams, it goes faster.

Coach Sullivan taught him to throw a split-finger fastball. "Well, it's not exactly a split-finger; it's not the same as the split-finger a major league pitcher throws. My fingers aren't big enough to grip the ball for a real split-finger. What I do is grip the ball along the seams where they're closest together. I use an overhand delivery, the same as for my regular fastball.

"My split-finger distracts the batter. With my regular fastball, which the batter is used to seeing, it's kind of difficult to make out the seams. But the rotation of the split-finger is entirely different. All the batter sees is seams."

Tom Mineo's basic advice for any young pitcher is to always do your best. Never let up. "I used to ease up on the batter when I got behind in the count. On 3 and 0, say, I'd sometimes throw the ball slower than I normally do—and the batter would smack it. Nowadays I always bear down."

STEVEN MAZZARIELLO

Shortstop Second Base Pitcher

Steven Mazzariello plays shortstop and second base, also pitches.

A slick fielder and an outstanding hitter, 12-year-old Steven Mazzariello got his first taste of baseball by playing catch with his mom in the backyard. He was six. Then his dad took over, and he and Steven started tossing the ball back and forth on a regular basis. "He also threw me grounders and high pops," says Steven.

Not long after, Steven began playing tee ball. That's how he

Name: **Steven Mazzariello**
Nickname: **Mazz**
Age: **12**
Height: **4′ 10″** Weight: **75**
Bats: **Right** Throws: **Right**
Team: **Cardinals; East Longmeadow, Massachusetts**
Position: **Shortstop, Second Base, Pitcher**
Other Sports: **Golf, Basketball**
Favorite Uniform Number: **8**
Favorite Big League Team: **Boston Red Sox**
Favorite TV Program: **"The Wonder Years"**
Hobbies: **Collecting baseball cards**

learned to hit. He played tee ball for a year before moving up the ladder to a baseball league for 8-to-10-year-olds.

When Steven first faced "live" pitching, he remembers being a little bit afraid at the plate. "But on my second time at bat, I got a triple," he says. "And on my next time at bat, I singled. After that, I wasn't afraid anymore. When I go to bat now, all I think about is getting a hit."

Today, Steven and his dad, the assistant principal at the local high school, play catch frequently. "And lots of times," says Steven, "we'll go over to the school field, and he'll pitch and I'll hit. And he'll also hit me grounders."

Steven is very serious about baseball. To strike out or misplay a ball in the field disturbs him deeply.

His coach praises him for his skills, saying, "He has about the 'softest' hands I've ever seen. And for his size, he has a very strong arm."

The coach adds, "Steven could be a *real* good baseball player some day—if he stays with it." Steven does look forward to

Hold the bat out like this for five seconds. If your arm shakes, the bat is too heavy for you.

playing baseball in high school and perhaps in college. After that, he's not sure.

Steven is lead-off batter on his team. He's knowledgeable about equipment and offers some pointers about it.

"You don't want a bat that's too heavy. I use a 30-inch bat that weighs 22 ounces. To find out whether your bat's weight is OK, hold the bat out straight for five seconds. If your arm shakes, the bat's too heavy for you."

The correct length of the bat is important, too. Tom checks his by taking his stance at the plate and swinging the bat back and forth. "As you swing, the bat should cover the outside edge of the plate," says Tom. "If it doesn't, you need a longer bat." The diameter of the handle shouldn't be too thick. "You want a handle you can grip tightly, or you're not going to be able to hit solidly. And the bat will sting your fingers when you hit a fastball."

How you grip the bat makes a difference. Steven feels that choking-up a little bit makes the bat easier to swing. "Try choking-up only half an inch or so. You'll be able to get the bat around faster. That's why coaches tell you to choke-up when the count goes to two strikes; it makes it easier to make contact."

Steven wears two batting gloves to get a better grip. "When the ball happens to hit the bat on the handle, and you get a lot of vibration, wearing two gloves helps prevent the bat from stinging your fingers."

Steven is known for getting hits, and has this advice for others who want to improve their hitting. "You shouldn't try to kill the ball. You shouldn't try to see how far you can hit it. Step into the pitch and hit hard, but only try to meet the ball. Do that and you'll get your extra-base hits."

He uses a closed stance because it feels more comfortable for him. Waiting for the pitch, his knees are slightly bent, his weight evenly balanced, his eyes on the pitcher. "As the ball comes in and your arms go back, it's important not to drop your hands," he says. "Otherwise, you won't have a level swing. Be sure to keep the swing level. Keep your shoulders level; don't drop your back shoulder. Watch the ball until it hits the bat. Swing through the ball."

Steven watches major league baseball on television. "You can learn a lot about hitting by watching major league players. You can learn about a level swing by watching Wade Boggs [of the

When you swing, swing through the ball.

As the pitcher delivers the ball, you're concentrating on the batter, ready to move in any direction.

Boston Red Sox]. You can also see how he tries to go with the pitch. If the pitch is outside, Boggs [a left-handed hitter] tries to go to right field with it. If the pitch is inside, Boggs tries to pull it. I try to hit like Boggs. I know that if you try to pull an outside pitch, the chances are you'll ground out. So I try to go to right field with it. I also watch Mike Greenwell [Boston Red Sox], Kirby Pickett [Minnesota Twins], and Don Mattingly [New York Yankees]."

Steven also watches runners on TV and likes the split screen that shows the pitcher and the runner at the same time. "You can see how the runner works on the pitcher. You can learn a lot from runners like Ellis Burks [Boston Red Sox] and Eric Davis [Cincinnati Reds]. I like to watch how major league players run the bases, too. They keep their heads down and run full tilt. They don't look for the ball. They always run aggressively, trying to take the extra base. Pete Rose was like that."

Steven has played every infield position except third base. Shortstop is the position he prefers. "I like it because a lot more hits go to shortstop, and you get to make more throws." Steven has a very good arm, so the long throw to first base is no problem for him.

His positive attitude helps his game. "You should believe you can get any ball that's hit in your direction," he says. "Go for it. Try for anything you can."

At shortstop, he has to know the game situation at all times, and it helps to know the batters. He adjusts his position, depending on who is at the plate. Who is pitching can make a difference, too.

"We have a pitcher named Mike St. Clair, who throws real fast. When he's pitching, the batters have trouble getting the bat around; they're always hitting late. With a right-handed batter at the plate, the ball is more likely to go to the right side when Mike is pitching. So I move more toward second base. And when there's a pitcher who is not so fast, you play the batters to pull more or hit up the middle.

"On bunts, I move in. If there's a steal attempt and there's a leftie at bat, I know I'm going to be the one covering second base, so I have to be ready for that.

"You have to know in advance where you're going to go with

the ball if it comes to you. Suppose there's a runner on second and I catch a line drive. Then I'm going to try to double up the runner. If it's a ground ball with a runner on first, I'm going to throw to second to try for a double play."

His coach taught Steven about "soft" hands. "He means my hands shouldn't be stiff; they should 'give' when the ball arrives. It's important to be relaxed, not to hurry. Make sure your throw is good."

Steven tries to charge every ball. That's not always possible. On a one-hopper that hits close to him, he may have to back up a step. He tries to get in front of line drives. "Line drives below my waist, I catch with the fingers of my glove pointing downward. Those that are above my waist, I catch with my fingers pointing up."

On balls hit to his right or left, he moves with a crossover step. To get a ball hit to his left, he crosses his right foot in front of his left. "If I can't get in front of the ball, I stretch out and backhand it." On pop flies, he backpedals, then comes in on the ball to make the catch.

As the shortstop, he sometimes has to be the cutoff man, relaying an outfielder's throw to the right base. "I put my hands over my head and yell so the outfielder can spot me quickly. Naturally, you have to know the game situation and where the runners are headed; otherwise, you're not likely to throw to the right base."

On throws to first, most players aim at the first baseman's chest. Not Steven. "I aim for his head, because I know the ball will drop down and arrive at his chest."

When playing shortstop, you have to back up the third baseman when he fields ground balls. With a runner on base, the shortstop may have to back up the pitcher when the catcher returns the ball to him. And the shortstop and second baseman

Reach out and backhand balls hit to your left.

have to back up each other on attempted steals. When he covers for the second baseman, Steven straddles the base, facing the runner, and puts his glove down in front of the base. "Let the runner slide into it," he says. "If there's not time enough to get the glove down, try a sweep tag."

On run-down plays, he knows that the idea is to throw the ball as few times as possible. "Chase the runner and tag him out; throw only when you have to. Every time you throw, there's a chance the ball will be dropped and the runner will escape. Don't fake your throw too often, either. You can fake out the guy you expect to catch the ball. Keep it simple. You should get the runner every time."

STEVEN BAEZ ROSARIO

Shortstop
Outfield
Pitcher

Steven is a long-ball hitter who likes to pull the ball.

Hard-hitting Steven Baez Rosario first got interested in baseball through television. His dad, a fan of the New York Yankees, liked to tune in their games. When Steven was about three years old, he began watching, too. "He started imitating some of the things the players were doing, the way they'd hit or catch a ball," Steven's father recalls. "And he picked up a lot of baseball terms. That's how he got to like the game."

When Steven was about five, his father began taking him to

Name: **Steven Baez Rosario**
Nickname: **Steve**
Age: **12**
Height: **5′ 2″** Weight: **110**
Bats: **Right** Throws: **Right**
Team: **Hurricanes; Bronx, New York**
Position: **Shortstop, Outfield, Pitcher**
Other Sports: **Football, Basketball**
Favorite Uniform Number: **23**
Favorite Big League Team: **New York Yankees**
Favorite TV Program: **"Alf"**
Hobbies: **Skateboarding, Bike riding, Roller skating**

a park not far from the family's Upper Manhattan apartment to teach him how to catch and hit. According to Steven's father, they played with a tennis ball, a rubber ball, a Wiffle ball, or "just about anything that was round."

At first, Steven was frustrated because he couldn't hit the ball with the ease of the big league players he had been watching on television. "It took a lot of patience," says Steven's father, "for both of us."

Steven's first experience with organized baseball wasn't a happy one. The coaches weren't as patient and understanding as Steven's father had been. They yelled at him and the other players whenever they made mistakes. Steven didn't like that. He dropped out of the program.

Although Steven wasn't playing on a team, he continued to develop his baseball skills. On weekends he and his father practiced in the park. And Steven and his friends played stickball or Wiffle ball in the streets after school and during summer vacations. They played almost every day.

"We play a whole block," Steven says. "There are as many as five kids to a team. You use the same rules as in baseball."

Both sides of the street are lined with parked automobiles. Car wheels serve as first and third base. One sewer is home plate. Another is second base.

Players have to keep watch for street traffic. But it's not an important concern. "When a car comes, we just move out of the way," Steven says.

When Steven was 12, he joined the Hurricanes, one of the teams in a four-team league sponsored by the Love Gospel

Steven likes playing for the Hurricanes. "The coaches don't criticize you or pressure you," he says.

Not only powerful at the plate, Baez has a strong arm, too.

Assembly. From the beginning, it was an enjoyable experience for him. "The coaches and the players didn't criticize us," Steven says. "They didn't put you under a lot of pressure."

Powerfully built, Steven is one of his team's most dependable long-ball hitters. Here's what he has to say about hitting:

"My favorite hitter in major league baseball is Don Mattingly of the Yankees. But I don't bat like Mattingly does. I have my own style. Whenever I try to hit the ball like someone else, I just strike out a lot.

"I use an aluminum bat because wood bats hurt my hands when I hit, even when I have a tight grip. And with an aluminum bat, the ball goes farther for me. The bat I use weighs 24 ounces and is 31 inches long.

"I don't think it's difficult to hit a ball. When you go up to the plate, take your time. Be relaxed. Keep your eye on the ball. When you take your eye off the ball, you can swing too early or too late; you miss the ball. You've got to concentrate.

"Fastballs right down the middle, not high, not low, are what I like. I'm a long-ball hitter who likes to pull the ball. I have a fast swing and lots of power, and when I hit a really fast fastball, it goes far."

At bat, Steven likes to let the first pitch go by. If that first pitch is a ball, he usually takes the second pitch, too. "The next pitch is the key pitch," he says. "If it's another ball, I know the pitcher is wild and I'm probably going to be walked. But if the third pitch is a strike, I get set to hit the next pitch. I know it's probably going to be a good one."

When the first pitch is a strike, he always swings at the next pitch. If he misses, making the count 0 and 2, he knows the pitcher will waste the third pitch, that it will be a ball. "But the next pitch, the fourth pitch, will be a strike, so I get ready to swing.

"In our league I can hit every pitcher, and I don't strike out very much. But one time this season, I struck out three times in one game. I don't know what happened."

Steven plays shortstop for the Hurricanes. "It's a hard position to play," he says. "You have to concentrate. You can't be looking at other things. You have to concentrate on the ball."

On ground balls, Steven gets in front of the ball, bends low, and keeps his glove down. "If you don't catch the ball and make the play, at least you'll stop it. That's what my coach told me." He used to hold the glove too high on grounders and made a lot of errors. "The ball would pop out of my glove or go under it."

On run-down plays, he can move fast. If a runner is trapped between second and third, and he has the ball, he chases the runner toward third. If the runner doesn't stop, he throws to the third baseman. "Then I run right past the third baseman to back him up and cover third base. The second baseman has come over to take the throw, if the third baseman doesn't tag the runner out."

When the pitcher or catcher throws to first and catches the runner off base, the first baseman chases the runner toward second, then throws the ball to the second baseman. "It's my job to back up the second baseman."

According to Steven, the hardest play for a shortstop is a double play when the ball is grounded to the second baseman. "You have to start for the base fast to cover it and take the second baseman's throw. You have to time it so you arrive at the base at the same time the ball does. You catch the ball, step on the base with your left foot as you throw to first. You have to have a good arm and you have to throw fast."

ALAN HUBBARD

Catcher
Pitcher

Catcher Alan Hubbard also pitches occasionally.

Confident, determined, a take-charge player, 12-year-old Alan Hubbard, a catcher, has been playing baseball since he was six, and before that he played a year of tee ball. Tall and with a blocky build, a catcher is what Alan looks like.

Alan has played several positions, including pitcher, shortstop, catcher, center field, and first base. Catching is the position he likes the best. "I don't know exactly why," he says, "but I've

Name: **Alan Hubbard**
Nickname: **Hub, Hubby**
Age: **12**
Height: **5′** Weight: **125**
Bats: **Right** Throws: **Right**
Team: **Cardinals; East Longmeadow, Massachusetts**
Position: **Catcher, Pitcher**
Other Sports: **Hockey, Soccer**
Favorite Uniform Number: **14**
Favorite Big League Team: **Boston Red Sox**
Favorite TV Program: **"NHL Hockey Playoffs"**
Hobbies: **Drawing, Collecting baseball cards, Watching TV sports**

always liked positions that are defensive. In hockey, I'm a goaltender. In soccer, I'm a goalie. I'm always defensive."

Alan also enjoys being the catcher because it puts him in charge. "I like that," he says. "I call the pitches, telling the pitcher whether to put the ball inside or outside. I call pitchouts.

"And there are certain plays I'm in charge of calling. Suppose the team we're playing has runners on first and third and no one is out or there's one out. The runner on first breaks for second, attempting to steal. When I see that happening, I yell out, 'Steve, here it comes!' Then, instead of throwing to the second baseman who's covering second, I gun the ball to Steve Mazzariello, our shortstop. The runner on third, thinking I've thrown to second, and there's going to be a play there, breaks for home plate. Then Mazzariello fires the ball back to me, and we get the runner at home."

Alan's status on the Cardinals is unusual because his father is the team's coach. Is this an advantage or a disadvantage for him?

It can work either way, he says. "One advantage is that if someone else is catching, he'll let me play some other position. Maybe he'll put me in center field or I might even pitch. But I don't sit on the bench."

One disadvantage is that as the team's No. 1 catcher he can get overworked during a game. "There are times he won't let me come out from behind the plate," Alan says. "Sometimes I've felt like I've caught for a hundred innings in a row. If it happened to another kid back there, he'd give him a break."

Alan seems big enough and strong enough to cope with occasional weariness. And also with the lumps all catchers must suffer. In tournament play one season, Alan was bowled over by a runner—"a real big kid"—when he attempted to block home plate. "I held onto the ball," he says with pride.

And the same season, a batter fouled a ball off the inside of Alan's knee, where there's no padding. But Alan stayed in the game.

"I don't mind these things," Alan says. "I'm used to getting banged up from hockey."

If you want to be a catcher and not get hurt, Alan advises never turning your back on the ball. "Remember, all of your equipment is in front of you," he says. "When you turn your back on the ball, you're unprotected."

Here are some other tips he has:

"When I get in position to give the target to the pitcher, I squat down, keeping my feet comfortably apart. My feet are flat to the ground. I rest my left forearm on my left leg. I keep my right hand, my bare hand, down by my right foot so it won't get hit by a foul tip.

"When you get in position behind the batter, and you're not sure whether you're the right distance from the batter, put out your right arm; your hand should just touch the batter. In other

Hubbard gives a target to his pitcher.

words, you're supposed to be an arm's length away from the batter.

"You also can get some idea of the distance by checking the batter's grip. When I see the batter is choking-up, I know I can move a little bit closer—and I do. I like to get close to the plate."

One of the first things Alan learned when he started catching was how to "frame" the ball. This means quickly bringing a pitch that might be a ball into the strike zone after you've caught it. This can influence the way the umpire calls the pitch.

"You don't have to move your whole hand when you frame the pitch," says Alan. "It's all in the wrist. After you've got the ball in your glove, you just bend or twist your wrist to the right or left, up or down. It's simple to do, but once in a while you can earn the pitcher a strike on a pitch that should have been a ball."

On his team, the catcher doesn't use signs because the pitchers throw only fastballs and change-ups. The coach doesn't want the pitchers throwing curves because, as Alan puts it, "curves mess up your arm." The pitcher throws whatever pitch he wants to throw, fastball or change-up. "I just give him a target—inside, outside, or down the middle; I just tell him where to put it."

But Alan knows how to give signs. He positions his glove slightly below his left knee, with the back of the glove facing the third base coach. This prevents the coach from stealing the sign. "Then you put down one finger or two, whatever the sign happens to be."

When a pitch bounces in the dirt in front of the plate, Alan blocks it. "What I do is drop down to my knees, using my equipment to do the blocking. I bend my chest toward the ground, so that if the ball bounces off my chest protector, it will fall right in front of me. And I always keep my head down, putting my chin on my chest. This is so the ball, when it bounces up, won't hit me in the throat." If the ball is thrown in the dirt to the left or right of him, he moves in that direction to keep the ball in front of him.

When there's a runner on first who attempts to steal, and Alan has the ball, he rises up and brings the ball up next to his ear. "Then I take a step and snap the throw toward second. I try to put the ball right on the target, right in front of the base, so all the fielder has to do is make the catch and put the ball down.

"When I throw, I don't aim for second base. If I did that, it would be a lollipop of a throw. Instead, I aim for the pitcher's

Alan knows how to conceal sign from third base coach.

Throws to bases have to be snap throws.

head. He's standing in front of the mound. He moves out of the way to the right or left.

"Because I'm right-handed, I sometimes have a problem throwing to the bases when a left-handed batter is at the plate. For instance, when I go to throw the ball to first, I have to be careful that I don't hit the batter in the head. I have to move to my left before throwing."

On bunt plays, Alan fields the ball with both his glove and his bare hand—unless he knows the runner is very fast. "Then," he says, "I'll pick up the ball bare-handed and gun it to first."

When one of the fielders makes the play on a bunt attempt, it is up to Alan as catcher to shout out directions for where the ball should go—first, second, or third. "I don't shout the number only once; I yell it out three or four times."

On foul pop-ups, his catcher's mask can be a problem. "That's because the mask I use is attached to the helmet," he explains, "and it's hard to get the whole thing off quickly. In major league baseball, the mask is separate from the helmet, so it's much easier to flip off the mask. When the ball goes up, I slide the mask over my head, and drop it and the helmet as I go for the ball.

"In our league, foul balls don't go very high into the air. By the time I get my mask and helmet off, about all I can do is dive for the ball."

On plays at home plate, with the runner coming toward him, Alan tries to face the runner, keeping his left foot on the foul line. "After I make the tag, I'm supposed to move toward the pitcher's mound. This prevents you from getting run over.

"I don't always do this, however. Once I get the ball, I like to block the plate and let the runner slide into me.

"I always keep the ball in my mitt, and squeeze it. I make the tag with the front side of the mitt. If you try tagging with the back side of the mitt, it's easier for the runner to knock the ball loose."

CHRIS CONWAY

Second Base

On ground balls, be sure to get down low; use both hands.

When Chris Conway was three years old, his mom used to take him to a local field to watch his dad play softball. Chris wanted to try the game himself. Since he was a little bit too young for the standard equipment, his dad bought him a Wiffle ball and a plastic bat. Chris, his sister, who is two years older than he is, and their dad often played Wiffle ball together.

When he was five, Chris advanced to tee ball. "You're sup-

Name: **Christopher Conway**
Nickname: **Chris**
Age: **11**
Height: **4′ 7″** Weight: **70**
Bats: **Right** Throws: **Right**
Team: **Cardinals; East Longmeadow, Massachusetts**
Position: **Second Base**
Other Sports: **Basketball, Soccer**
Favorite Uniform Number: **1**
Favorite Big League Team: **Cincinnati Reds**
Favorite TV Program: **"Growing Pains," "Wide World of Sports"**
Hobbies: **(none)**

posed to be six to play tee ball," Chris says, "but I knew the coach so he let me on the team."

Because of his Wiffle ball experience, Chris was a good hitter but he had problems fielding the ball. His dad helped him. In practice sessions, Mr. Conway would throw grounders and pop flies to Chris. "That helped me a lot," he says. Chris played tee ball for three years before moving up to a baseball league, for 8-to-10-year-olds.

Beginning with his tee ball days, Chris has played in the outfield as well as the infield. Second base is his best position. "There's more action there. More hits come to you and you get to take throws from the infield," he says.

Chris's favorite major league team is the Cincinnati Reds. His favorite infielder is Chris Sabo, who plays shortstop and third base for the Reds. His favorite outfielder is Cincinnati's Eric Davis.

But it's not easy to live in East Longmeadow, Massachusetts, and be a fan of the Cincinnati Reds. Only a handful of Cincinnati games are televised locally. And all of Chris's friends root for the Mets or the Yankees. Chris's loyalty is constantly being tested.

He doesn't let that affect his performance, though. He's good at second base because he knows what it takes to play that position well. Besides having to be aware of the game situation at all times, Chris says that you have to know what options you have when the ball comes to you. "Do you throw the runner out at first, try to tag the runner going to second, go for a double play by tossing the ball to the shortstop? Or, if the bases are loaded, do you touch second base for a force or do you throw home?

"What you want to do is make the smart play. If there's a runner on first with one out or no outs and the batter hits a ground ball to you, the smart play is to go to second for a double play. Using your head is important. Don't worry about mistakes; everyone makes them."

When Chris first started playing second, the ball sometimes went right through his legs. "I wasn't getting my glove down low enough. The other guys on the team got a little mad at me. They said to me, 'You gotta get in front of the ball. You gotta get down more. You gotta put the glove down.' Now I bend my knees, get down low, and put my glove down all the way, and I use both hands. The ball doesn't go through my legs anymore."

To play second base, you have to be able to pick up grounders and throw quickly. "When a ball is hit to me and the play is at first, I take a quick look at the runner to see how much time I have. If the runner is fast, I may have to snap the throw. But if there's no reason to hurry, I don't; I take my time.

"On plays at first base, I don't have a long throw to make, so I don't throw hard. I target on the first baseman's chest.

"The same on double plays. When I throw to the shortstop, I don't throw the ball hard. I use a sidearm throw. If I'm real close

It's important to get rid of the ball quickly, but don't rush.

to the shortstop, I toss the ball underhand. After I make the throw, I duck down. I don't want to get hit by the shortstop's throw to first base."

Chris always uses both hands to catch pop flies, and he watches the ball until it hits his glove. If the sun is a problem, he uses his hand to screen out the sun. "Then, at the last second, I take the hand away because I want to catch the ball with both hands. That way I can get the ball out of the glove fast to make the throw."

On pop flies that come between Chris and the outfielder, he usually lets the outfielder take it. Since he is coming in, it's easier for him to make the catch.

As the second baseman, Chris has to act as the cutoff man on balls hit to the outfield. He runs out to take the outfielder's throw and relay it to the right base. "The shortstop and I give one another directions on cutoff plays," he says. "When I go out for the ball, the shortstop, who's covering second base, shouts instructions. He'll yell 'Cut two!' or 'Cut three!'—meaning that I should throw the ball to either second base or third base."

GLOSSARY

BALK—An illegal motion by the pitcher with one or more runners on base for which each base runner is advanced one base.

BATTER'S BOX—The lined-off area (5 1/2 by 3 feet, according to Little League rules, and 6 by 4 feet for major league play) within which the batter must remain during a turn at the plate.

CHANGE, CHANGE-UP—A slow pitch meant to fool the batter which is thrown with the same motion as a fastball.

CLEAN-UP HITTER—A powerful hitter who bats in fourth position in the team's batting order, and whose job it is to "clean" the bases should any or all of the first three batters get on base.

COUNT—The number of balls and strikes on the batter.

CUTOFF—For an infielder to intercept an outfielder's throw toward home plate or a base.

CUTOFF MAN—The player who acts to cut off a throw from an outfielder.

DOUBLE PLAY—A play in which two players are put out.

DOUBLE UP—To put out a base runner as the second out of a double play.

DRAG BUNT—A bunt made by a left-handed batter who "drags" the ball down the first base line in an effort to get a base hit.

FORCE, FORCE PLAY—A situation in which a base runner must attempt to reach the next base. On a force, a fielder has only to touch the base to put out the runner.

JAM—To pitch inside to a batter to prevent a full and powerful swing.

JUMP—When attempting to steal a base, the measure of advantage the runner gains over the pitcher by his lead and getaway move.

MOUND—*See* Pitcher's mound.

PICK-OFF—A quick throw by the pitcher or catcher in an attempt to catch a runner off base.

PITCHER'S MOUND—The slightly elevated portion of the infield which slopes to the level of the field and on which the pitcher stands to pitch the ball.

POP FLY, POP-UP—A high fly ball.

PULL THE BALL—For a right-handed hitter to hit to left field, or for a left-handed hitter to hit to right field.

RUBBER—The rectangular slab of white rubber, which measures 6 by 24 inches, and is set in the pitcher's mound. The pitcher must remain in contact with the rubber during the pitch and step off the rubber before attempting to pick off a runner.

RUNDOWN—A situation in which a base runner is trapped off base between two bases, while two or more fielders in the base paths toss the ball back and forth on an attempt to make the tag.

SACRIFICE, SACRIFICE BUNT—A bunt made with less than two outs that advances a base runner, and on which the batter is out.

SPLIT-FINGER FASTBALL—A fastball that drops down as it breaks to the right or left as it nears the plate. Professional players throw the pitch by gripping the ball in-between the forefinger and middle finger.

STRIKE-BOX—A square with an X in the center painted on the side of a building that serves much the same purpose as a home plate. A pitched ball that hits within the square is a strike. A pitch that misses the square is a ball.

SWITCH-HITTER—A batter who can bat either right-handed or left-handed.

TAG UP—To remain in contact with a base until after a fly ball is caught, with the idea of advancing to the next base.

TEE BALL—A game for 6-to-8-year-olds with rules similar to Little League baseball, but in which the ball is hit from a tall batting tee instead of being pitched.

WIFFLE BALL—A hollow, white plastic ball with eight oblong holes on one side; also a backyard version of baseball played with such a ball and using a plastic bat.

INDEX

Aaron, Hank, 50
Arm speed, 9, 79

Backpedal, 20, 72
Balk, 92
Base-running, 29, 30, 31, 43, 58, 71
Baseball camp, 18, 20, 30, 44; clinics, 8, 30, 44
Baseball cards, 8, 10, 17, 24, 44, 49, 57, 66
Bat, 36, 68; size, 67, 68, 78; weight, 67, 78; aluminum, 77, 78; wood, 77
Batter, 15, 27, 39, 46, 66, 67
Batter's box, 24, 51, 57, 92
Batting average, 27, 50, 56, 57
Batting cage, 17
Batting glove, 58, 68
Batting range, 45; robots, 45
Batting stance, 8, 18, 27, 36, 58, 60, 67, 68
Batting stride, 45
Boggs, Wade, 68, 70
Boston Red Sox, 10, 30, 38, 66, 70, 71, 81
Braintree, Massachusetts, 38
Bronx, New York, 23, 24, 25, 48
Bunt, 28, 29, 30, 32, 35, 36, 45, 46, 71, 86
Burks, Ellis, 71

Campbell, Pat, 16–22
Catcher, 14, 28, 29, 30, 44, 62, 72, 80, 81, 82, 83; frame the ball, 83, 84; blocking plate, 84, 86
Catcher's mask, 86
Center fielder, 18, 20, 37, 38, 39, 48, 50, 53, 80, 82
Cincinnati Reds, 71, 88, 89
Clean-up hitter, 43, 92
Clemens, Roger, 10, 13
Coach, 8, 9, 10, 17, 18, 20, 30, 32, 37, 42, 53, 57, 58, 60, 62, 64, 66, 68, 72, 75, 77, 78, 81, 82, 84; signs, 32, 35, 52
Conway, Chris, 87–91
Count, 92
Crossover step, 72
Cutoff man, 7, 22, 42, 72, 91, 92

Davis, Eric, 71
Desilets, Dan, 37–42

Double play, 7, 32, 72, 79, 89, 92
Drag bunt, 7, 18, 92
Dykstra, Lenny, 51

East Longmeadow (Massachusetts) Cardinals, 7, 10, 17, 30, 38, 44, 57, 66, 81, 88
East Longmeadow, Massachusetts, 38, 88

Fielder, 25, 27, 28, 30, 43, 44, 58
First baseman, 28, 43, 44, 46, 60, 72, 79, 80, 89
Force play, 92

Gladiators, Bronx, New York, 24, 49, 51, 53
Greenwell, Mike, 70
Ground ball, 14, 25, 27, 31, 32, 42, 43, 44, 46, 50, 53, 60, 65, 66, 72, 78, 79, 89

Hellyer, Pat, 29–36
Henderson, Rickey, 8
Hidden-ball trick, 31
Hitter, 19, 20, 43, 44, 51, 56, 68, 77; line drives, 20; contact hitter, 27, 51, 56
Hobbies, 10, 17, 24, 30, 38, 44, 49, 57, 66, 75, 81

Infield, 16, 20, 28, 37, 71
Infielder, 18, 25, 39, 53
Instruction video, 8, 55

Jam, 60, 62, 92
Johnson, Howard, 27

Karavish, Brian, 43–47

Left field, 16, 38, 55
Line drive, 7, 47, 72

Mattingly, Don, 8, 18, 70, 77
Mays, Willie, 50, 51
Mazzariello, Steven, 65–73, 81
Mineo, Tom, coach, 7
Mineo Tom, Jr., 7, 56–64
Minnesota Twins, 70
Montreal Expos, 24

New York Giants, 51
New York Mets, 24, 27, 49, 50, 89
New York Yankees, 8, 17, 18, 44, 57, 70, 74, 77, 89

Outfielder, 16, 18, 19, 31, 37, 39, 42, 50, 53, 60, 72, 74, 75, 91; mistakes, 42

Perez, Marcus, 49
Perez, Seneca, 48–55
Philadelphia Phillies, 51
Pick-off, 92
Pickett, Kirby, 70
Pine tar, 58
Pitcher, 9–15, 23, 26, 39, 43, 46, 50, 51, 53, 55, 57, 60–64, 65, 66, 75, 78, 79, 80, 81, 82, 89; sidearm, 39, 60, 89; windup, 13, 60
Pitches, types of: change-up, 12, 14, 15, 64, 84, 92; curveball, 53, 64, 84; fastball, 9, 12, 13, 53, 57, 64, 78; grip, 13, 14, 55, 64; inside, 14, 19, 24, 51, 62, 70; outside, 14; slider, 13; split-finger, 64
Pitchout, 81
Pop-up flies, 22, 50, 65, 86, 88, 91, 93

Ramirez, Omar, 23–28
Roberts, Dr. Glyn C., 7
Robinson, Jackie, 51
Rosario, Steven Baez, 74–79
Rose, Pete, 71
Rubber, 93
Rundown plays, 79, 93

Sabo, Chris, 88
St. Clair, Mike, 9–15, 71
Second baseman, 23, 27, 37, 38, 46, 49, 50, 65, 72, 73, 79, 88–91
Shortstop, 9, 10, 18, 27, 65, 71, 72, 74, 78, 79, 80, 81, 89, 91
Sliding, 31, 32, 35, 36, 47, 86
Springfield (Massachusetts) College, 30
Stealing, 30, 32, 35, 45, 46, 47, 71, 73, 81
Stickball, 7, 75
Strike-box, 24, 25, 93
Strike zone, 83
Sullivan, Jack, coach, 60, 64
Sweep tag, 47, 73
Swing, 15, 16, 17, 27, 52, 68, 78
Switch hitter, 25, 27, 93

Tag up, 32, 93
Tee ball, 10, 65, 66, 80, 86, 88, 93
Television, 7, 44, 45, 58, 62, 71, 74, 89
Television, favorite program, 10, 17, 24, 30, 38, 44, 49, 57, 66, 75, 81, 88
Third baseman, 16, 17, 18, 19, 20, 23, 43, 44, 45, 46, 50, 60, 72, 79, 91; qualifications, 45
Throwing: overhand, 22, 36, 37, 46, 60; sidearm, 22, 39, 60, 86, 89; underhand, 17, 46

Umpire, 83
University of Illinois, 7
University of Texas, 13

Vartas, Michael, 23, 24, 25

Wiffle ball, 7, 10, 18, 25, 30, 44, 75, 87, 93